Neighborhood Playthings Collection

A Trio of Very Sexy Erotic Stories

M.C. Plains

CONTENTS

A spontaneous night out.
A spicy swingers story.
Unintended
Playthings
M.C. Plains

Story One: Unintended Playthings

I saw them staring at us from across the room. Well, staring was probably not the right word. More like looking, glancing... observing. They were an attractive couple, a man and a woman about our age, sitting at the opposite side of the horseshoe-shaped bar. She was petite, hair cut into a neat bob with highlights that complimented her bronze, sun-kissed skin.

She was dressed up for a night out, in a black dress that hugged her curves and revealed a hint of cleavage that we could see from where we sat. She had large, intense eyes with a slightly smoky shadow and a bright red lipstick that parted frequently to expose a mouthful of pearly white, very straight teeth when she smiled and laughed.

The man with her was tall, with an angular jaw and what looked from a distance to be green-grey eyes. He had a very sexy, intense look about him. He wore a button-up shirt with the top couple of buttons undone, revealing a smooth and tanned chest underneath. His shirt was rolled up at the ends revealing muscular forearms that looked strong and contoured like he maybe spent a lot of time working with his hands. Together, they were a magnetic duo and I was having a hard time keeping my eyes off them. I thought I had noticed them look over at us once or twice as well, but the bartender was doing things in the middle of the bar, and I figured they could have been glancing his way while he made drinks. I was actively trying not to stare despite them having much of my attention.

I placed my hand on my husband's, and glancing at me, he followed my gaze to where they sat. 'I've noticed you looking over there. What are you thinking about?' He asked.

'I know we haven't done this before... but they look like fun. What do you think?'

'I think that could be a fun way to spend the evening. Something to explore further, at least,' he said.

We summoned the bartender over. He wiped his hands on a bar towel and walked over to stand in front of us. 'What can I get for you?'

'That couple, over there. What are they drinking?'

'They're enjoying our signature cocktail, it's a riff on a Gin Rickey. With a chartreuse float.'

'That sounds delicious. We'll take one each,' he said, looking at me. I nodded in response. 'And please get them another round, on us,' gesturing at the couple. The bartender nodded. I saw him ring up the drinks on the register where my husband had opened a tab, and then we watched as he expertly created four spectacular-looking cocktails.

Bringing our two over to us first, he said, 'two Gin Rickey riffs. Enjoy. I'll take them theirs shortly.' We nodded and thanked him. I looked at my husband and took a sip. The warm liquor spilled down my throat, the herbaceous chartreuse causing my tastebuds to tingle. 'Mmm, good choice,' I said. My husband nodded. 'I like it as well, they seem to have good taste.'

We watched as the bartender took the other two drinks to the couple across the bar. He said something to them, presumably sharing where they were coming from, and we watched as the couple accepted the drinks, both smiling. The bartender left to look after other patrons, and the couple looked over at us and raised their glasses in cheers. We returned the gesture and took another sip of our drinks.

'That's a good sign,' I said, to which my husband nodded.

'Now we wait,' he replied.

We continued on with our conversation from earlier, chatting about the day and plans for our upcoming vacation, which we were very much looking forward to.

As we chatted, I considered the situation. My husband and I were fairly adventurous when it came to the bedroom. There had been times when we had introduced other parties to our bedroom—usually a woman, every now and then a man—but we had never played with a couple before. It had always intrigued me, and it just hadn't happened yet. As I eyed the couple over the other side of the bar, I wondered about what it would feel like, to have yet another sexy person and their various appendages involved. It seemed like when there were three people involved it was a group activity, whereas with four it felt like you could end up with various configurations of couples who paired off and went their separate ways. It's not something I'd spent a lot of time considering the mechanics of, but as it played out in my mind I found myself becoming increasingly turned on. Trying not to get overly flustered in the bar, I tried to focus my attention on what my husband was saying to me.

Chapter Two

A few minutes later, I sensed people approaching. It was too loud to hear footsteps over the bar's fairly loud music. A sensual voice said, 'Mind if we sit here?' It was the female from the couple across the way, and the man approached alongside her. They were both even more attractive up close than they had been from the other side of the bar. 'Yes, join us,' I said, gesturing to the stools beside us.

We started chatting and the couple introduced themselves. Their names were Jenny and Rick, and they were visiting from out of town for the weekend. They, like us, were foodies who also liked to try out trendy bars when they were on vacation. We had plenty to talk about, and they seemed like a genuinely nice couple, who also happened to be exceptionally attractive.

The drinks continued to flow as easily as the conversation, and we were all having a nice time, enjoying each other's company in this trendy bar.

After a while, I leaned over and whispered in Jenny's ear, "Want to go chat?"

She nodded. "We'll be right back," she said, taking my hand, and leading me towards the woman's restrooms.

"So what's the deal," she asked, as we entered the room. It was expansive, and we were the only ones in there, so we stood by the sinks to chat. "By the way, I think you're very attractive. And so is your husband. I just want to let you know that before we keep talking."

"Oh, well I think you're fucking sexy," I said, touching her arm gently. "And your husband is extremely easy on the eye. Not to mention, I've seen the way my husband looks at you. I think he's got a little crush."

She laughed warmly, her voice tinkling. "Want to play with us tonight? We have a nice hotel room."

"That sounds right up our alley," I said. "Count us in."

"Before we go back... were you and your husband planning this type of a night? I have to ask."

"No.. I mean, we weren't closed off to it. We just saw you across the bar and you... piqued our interest, you might say."

We were still the only ones in the restroom, and it felt a little risky, a little naughty, thinking about the chance of being caught if we decided to engage in... a little foreplay to get the night started. I stared at Jenny's voluptuous lips and pushed her against the wall next to the sink. I lifted her hands up to the wall, pinning her arms against it. She responded by smiling. "Oh, you like it like that, do you?"

'Mmmhmm,' I said, leaning forward and kissing her on the mouth.

She parted her beautiful red lips and we continued to make out, exploring with our tongues, just the right amount. The kiss felt just right, her lips soft and succulent, and I couldn't help but nibble on the lower one.

I let go of one of her wrists, and she reached down and caressed one of my breasts through my dress, fixating on my now-hard nipple and pinching it gently through the fabric. I moaned at her touch, little prickles of pleasure emanating across my upper half.

I reached down and lifted my hand up underneath her skirt, sliding it up her inner thigh. I slid it up until I hit resistance, and realized that she wasn't wearing underwear. 'You naughty girl,' I said. She smiled and laughed, desire in her eyes as I began rubbing at her exposed pussy.

'I knew I wouldn't be wearing them for long, so what's the point of pretending?' She said. 'Besides, less laundry.' We both laugh, and I continued to rub my fingers against her. She moaned as I slid two fingers inside her and pressed my chest to hers as we kissed some more.

Just as things were starting to get really heated we heard the sound of voices approaching, and as the heavy door creaked open I quickly lowered my hand from underneath her dress and pulled the top of mine back on properly. By the time the door fully opened and other guests walked in, we were standing side by side in front of the sinks, and any one would have assumed we were just in there to adjust our outfits and wash our hands. Nobody would ever have guessed that moments before, we had been engaged in a steamy makeout session, nor that my fingers had been inside her. We nodded at the people who entered and made our way out of the restroom and back to our husbands, chatting and laughing along the way.

Chapter Three

'You okay there, you two?' Asked her husband. 'We thought you got lost, we were about to send a search party.'

My husband looked at me and I winked. A little smile played on his face. He could guess exactly what had been going on, and I knew that he more than approved. He had no issue with me getting a woman, or a man for that matter, warmed up for a night of fun.

He and Rick seemed to be getting along as well, although they were having a conversation rather than fingering each other. Jenny and me, I decided, were off to a better start.

'Well, I know you're enjoying your conversation and all,' said Jenny, smiling. 'But we're ready to get a move on and keep the party going elsewhere if you'd like to join us.'

The men didn't need to be asked twice. They both settled up their checks and escorted us out of the bar. My husband had his hand gently on my back, and as we walked out we looked at each other and he gave me a tender kiss on the mouth. He was such a wonderful, affectionate man. Sexy, too. Just like this couple. I couldn't wait to see what the rest of the night would bring.

'The hotel is just up the street. We can walk there pretty quickly, if that's okay with you two.' We happily agreed and continued to chat as we wandered up the street. We pointed out a few landmarks that they weren't familiar with. It turned out that this was their first time in our city, and they'd picked it on a whim from several potential vacation spots.

'I'm glad you chose this one. It's so nice to have met you both,' I said, smiling at Jenny and Rick. They returned my smile.

'Likewise,' said Rick.

Chapter Four

We entered their hotel room and it turned out to be an impressive suite with a magnificent view of the harbour. We could see several neighbourhoods from this vantage point, tall buildings and residential areas, parks and monuments. The room itself was very large, with a separate living room with a couch and coffee table, and an adjoining bedroom with a very large, very comfortable-looking bed. It looked like it would be excellent for sleeping in, but we weren't here for that.

Rick headed over to the wet bar and poured the four of us cocktails, and we went and sat on the couch. He turned on some speakers that played ambient music in the background.

'So, ladies,' said my husband, looking at each of us. 'Would I be right in assuming that you started without us?'

Jenny and I looked at each other and grinned. 'Maybe... how did you know?' She said, looking at him from beneath her eyelashes.

'I think you should bring us up to speed, show us where you left things off,' said Rick.

'Gladly,' I replied.

The men went and sat in the two side chairs, leaving the couch to me and Jenny. It seemed they were after a cocktail and a show to start with, and I was only too glad to accommodate their request. It seemed that Jenny was also happy as she pushed me back on the couch, straddling me and beginning to make out with me, our mouths exploring each other like we did before.

This time, however, she pulled the top of my dress down, exposing my breasts, my nipples immediately hardening under the cool air conditioning and the fact that this woman was sexy as hell. The two men looked on with interest as Jenny began to suck on my nipples while she fondled my breasts. I moaned as pleasureful surges rippled through me, radiating out from my very sensitive nipples.

'Very nice,' said my husband. 'I like this view. However—,' he looked at Rick, 'I don't know about you, Rick, but I'm feeling very hungry.'

Rick nodded in agreement, and they both came toward us and instructed us to sit up in front of them.

Rick placed himself squarely in front of me, and I was mesmerised by his gorgeous, intense eyes. He smiled, sexily and reached out to fondle my breast. I noticed my husband reach forward and kiss Jenny deeply, their tongues intertwining passionately as he also reached out and fondled one of her breasts.

Without any form of communication, the men instinctively both reached down and pulled our thighs apart, revealing that in fact, neither of us was wearing underwear. I saw Rick look at me in appreciation, and then he reached out his index finger and rubbed gently at my pussy, teasing my clit. He inserted two fingers inside me as he leaned forward to kiss me; I returned the kiss, hungrily. He was exceptional at kissing, as well as using his fingers. But as he said, he was feeling very hungry.

He slid my hips forward so that my pussy made contact with his face. He reached out his tongue, teasing me with it, letting it gently touch my pussy and then flicking around my clit. He then began to focus on the nerves of my clit, licking, increasing his cadence, up and down, and in a circular motion. I moaned and noticed my husband look up, his eyes lustful, as I noticed his own face buried in between Jenny's legs. He was exploring her crevices with his tongue as well. She looked at me and moaned.' Fuck, your husband is good at eating pussy.'

'So is yours,' I replied. I curled my legs around her husband's neck, pulling his face closer to me as he continued to pleasure me with his tongue. She did the same. I continued to ride his face until I came. Right around the same time, so did Jenny. We both arched our backs in ecstasy as pleasure seared through our bodies, making us warm all over and tingly to the touch. Her husband was cheeky and kept eating me as I pulsated against his tongue, eager for more. He backed away as my body slowly stopped pulsating, and my husband was finishing up with Jenny. I leaned over and he and I engaged in a long, slow tongue kiss. 'Mmm, she tastes wonderful,' I said.

My husband nodded. 'She does indeed.' Teasing, I leaned over and licked Jenny in one long, slow motion, from the top of her clit right down to her asshole. I pulled away and she smiled at me naughtily.

'I think it's about time to get our cocks sucked, what do you think?' My husband asked Rick, who nodded, desire still in his eyes.

They took our place on the couch next to each other and Jenny and I both dropped to our knees and leaned forward in front of Rick. We kissed along his sizeable endowment, one on either side, all the way along the length. Jenny began to suck on his cock and I reached under and started to pleasure his balls with my tongue. He groaned in pleasure, clearly enjoying the sensations of two sets of voluptuous lips on him. I sat back up and as Jenny swapped places with me to place her attention on her husband's balls, I looked over and saw him gently stroking his cock as he watched me and another woman put our mouths all over this other man.

'It'll be your turn soon,' I winked at him, and he smiled.

'Take your time, I'm enjoying the view,' he said, staring over at Jenny's round ass.

I continued to lick and suck Rick's cock and he gyrated his hips, thrusting into my mouth while Jenny pleasured his balls. I deep-throated him, allowing him to slide it in and out, in and out, while my husband watched my mouth envelop him.

Then it was my husband's turn. Jenny and I crawled over to him on all fours and Jenny immediately took my husband's hard cock in her mouth, guzzling it down her throat and letting him thrust it in and out. She then let me take it inside my mouth while she reached up and kissed him. We alternated, both pleasuring him with our mouths.

Before long, I looked at Jenny and we nodded at each other. It was time to be fucked by these two very sexy men. 'I want to watch you ride my husband's cock,' I said. I watched as Jenny climbed on my husband's lap and lifted one thigh over until she was straddling him. She slid her wet pussy down over him, and he pulled her down towards him until he slid inside her completely. She moaned and cried, 'Oh fuck, you feel amazing!' I realized I was a lucky wife, but looking over at her husband's cock, and having just had it all in my mouth, I realized that she wasn't doing too bad herself; his was certainly giving my husband's girth a run for its money. I climbed on top of her husband, lining his cock up with my pussy and lowered myself down firmly so that our groins connected. He moaned in pleasure as I slid over him, enveloping him.

We sat side by side and rode each other's husbands. The four of us made eye contact as Jenny and I bounced up and down on their hard cocks. I could see her breasts bouncing in the air, and my husband reached out to tweak her nipples as she rode him. She moaned in pleasure.

The men then directed us to get on our hands and knees on the couch. They swapped over and I felt the familiar but exciting feeling of my husband as he slid his cock deep inside me and thrust it in and out, in and out, while holding onto my hips. I looked over to my left and saw Rick plowing into Jenny with his girth, her breasts once again bouncing as he took her from behind. It was hard to explain, but my husband seemed extra assertive, extra in control of the situation as he thrust in and out of me. It was like having another man in the room was magnifying his dominance, and I liked it.

We then moved things to the bed, and it certainly was a big surface that easily fit all four of us. Within moments of hopping on we were a sea of arms and legs and big cocks and mouths and it was hard to keep track. At one stage I felt two cocks slamming into me at one time, and I also felt multiple tongues lapping at my pussy on more than one occasion. Nothing was planned, nothing was scripted, we just lost ourselves in the moment and let desire overcome us. I came at least three times and caused at least three orgasms with my hands, my pussy, and my mouth. Finally, we lay in a tangle on the bed, panting, glistening with sweat and saliva and all manner of fluids. It was a blissful mess, and I was feeling extremely satisfied.

Chapter Five

'You're welcome to spend the night, you two,' Jenny said. 'It's late, and the party doesn't need to stop quite yet.'

My husband looked at each other and smiled. We had found our kind of people.

We dozed off and awoke in the morning, when the sun was just starting to rise. We hadn't had more than a couple of hours of sleep, but we were tired and it had been restful. The bed had been as comfortable as I had predicted. I found myself between the two men, curled up in the nook of my husband's arm with one of my arms dangling over Rick's broad chest. I felt a pleasurable sensation down below and realized that Jenny had noticed me waking and had climbed down my body and was licking at my pussy with her tongue. She lapped at my emerging wetness and I moaned at this surprise little dose of pleasure first thing upon my waking up. Hearing my moan, the men both woke up and looked to see what was happening. 'Oh fuck yes,' said my husband, watching Jenny eating me out. 'What a way to start the day.' He moved to the end of the bed where Jenny's ass was propped up as she lay on all fours eating my pussy. He spread her asscheeks apart and began to fuck her from behind. Rick approached me, his hard dick unfurling in front of me, and I began to pleasure him with my mouth. He thrust his cock in between my lips, in and out, in and out, until he came. I swallowed as he pulled out, and he smiled and leaned down to kiss me.

Jenny moved up the bed and sat on my face, then, and I lapped at her pussy, and my husband slid into me behind her, and pounded me with his big hard cock while Rick watched, very pleased with the scene unfolding before him. My husband came with a loud, shuddering orgasm, and I licked Jenny's clit until she did as well, her back arching as my husband held onto her perky tits, squeezing her nipples hard as she orgasmed, causing her to yell out in pleasure.

Feeling like we had spent the perfect amount of time on this spontaneous getaway, my husband and I smiled at each other and nodded, and then proceeded to gather our clothes and dress while Rick and Jenny sat in the bed, nestled against each other. Once we were fully dressed, we grabbed our purse and wallet. They walked us to the door, still fully naked, and we kissed each of them, one by one. We headed out the door and walked the short distance back to our home.

Chapter Six

'Well,' I said to my husband as we wandered, enjoying the fresh morning sunshine on our faces. 'That wasn't quite how I was anticipating spending the evening. I thought we'd have one cocktail, maybe two, and be on our way.'

'I thought the same,' he said. 'But then I saw that insatiable mischievous look on your face and I knew we might be in for a different kind of night. A two-cocks-in-your-wifes-pussy, having-your-dick-sucked-by-a-sexy-stranger evening, if you will.'

'Would you rather we'd have stuck to our original plan,' I asked, looking up at him through my eyelashes with a little smile playing on my face.

'Absolutely fucking not,' exclaimed my husband.

'Me neither,' I said. We both laughed and he put his arm around me and kept it there, holding me tight for the rest of the walk back to our home.

THE END

Four women.
One very lucky man.
A stack of possibilities.

Stack of Pleasure
M.C. Plains

Story Two: Stack of Pleasure

I decided to get my husband a very special present for his 40th birthday. I was kind like that. And while I was known for my creative ideas, I think this one took the cake. I'd considered all of the usual suspects-- a naughty coupon book, some sexy lingerie for me to wear for him, a romantic dinner, some toys for the bedroom–but it felt like we had been there, done that. Not that our relationship had grown stale by any means–far from it. We had a healthy sex life and never tired of each other; however, I was feeling frisky and was open to coming up with something that would ensure the spice and spark that we both enjoyed would get a little refresher of sorts. Make that a big refresher, now that I think about it. One thing was for certain- he was not going to forget this gift. Ever.

Why did I put so much thought into this present– after all, some people think that birthday gifts are for children, something you grow out of. I like to think about this a bit differently. Life can be serious when you're grown up, with bills to pay and work to do. But someone's birthday is this one, glorious day, that you can choose to make all about that person. For that reason, I like to shower my husband with attention, and have found various ways to do it over the years. It seems to bring him joy, and so I keep doing it. Simple as that. We've been married for years now, and I actually care about making him feel happy. It feels good.

So that's why I've come up with this gift. Each year, it has to be bigger and better than the last. And at this point it feels like he has all of the things that he needs; but that said, he's never had this one thing. For this birthday, he's getting a stack.

A stack of vaginas. Or, put less crudely, four gorgeous women–all of his to explore. What a lucky man. Of course, this was fun for me as well. I enjoyed watching my husband being turned on by other women; I enjoyed following his gaze, the sparkle in his eye, the tightness in his pants. Some people viewed this type of ogling as disrespectful, but I found his fondness for the female form in all its beauty to very much be a turn-on, and one I intended to indulge in. I also enjoyed being able to touch, please and taste them myself. It was his birthday, so all attention would be on him; but if I got a chance to participate I would happily do so. ***

Of course, I wasn't going to tell him straight away, where's the fun in that? I was going to give him subtle clues leading up to the event. For a few weeks leading up to his birthday, I would neatly line things up in fours, an in-joke for my own benefit. He thought I was just being my quirky self. I'd casually mention the names of the women that would be coming to be his sexy playthings, as if they were old friends, and he didn't question it. He knew I had a wide circle of acquaintances from yoga and book club, pilates and cooking classes, so it wasn't uncommon for me to mention names that didn't sound as familiar as those of some of my closest friends. I intended for my clues to get less subtle leading up to the event.

It wasn't difficult to find the right women to do this with. I made friends easily, especially drinking acquaintances. I had identified three gorgeous ladies who were distant friends of friends, nobody that I had to see on a frequent basis–it was probably better that way for something like this. Just in case anything strange happened coming out of this, because as much as you try to just hope for the best, you never know how things will turn out. Luckily, attractive women were in plentiful supply in this town. I knew my husband's type–that was to say in a way that he didn't really have one. He liked tits, he liked ass, he liked a pretty face–beyond that, it didn't take much to get his interest. It was fun picking out a bit of an assortment for him to sample.

He had us lie on top of each other - I of course, got on top, where I belonged. He had us pose for a photo, and I'm so glad we did. There we were, lying on top of each other, pussies exposed, in a stack. What a fantasy come true for my husband, and for me. I couldn't wait to show my friends later. They hadn't believed that we were really going to do this.

I heard him put his phone down and suddenly felt a wet tongue caressing my pussy lips. I moaned as he licked back and forth, teasing my wetness. I was very aroused, laying atop this pile of beautiful women, their legs all spread for my husband's pleasure. We were all his playthings to do what he wanted with.

I couldn't see what was going on from here on out. Of course I could feel certain parts that involved me. It was exciting not seeing exactly what was going on. I think you should hear it from his perspective, seeing he got the full view.

The Husband

My wife was full of all sorts of ideas, but none had ever been quite as creative as this. She had surprised me with three women for my birthday–four including her, and I knew I was a very lucky man. I had been expecting a nice dinner, or maybe a clothing voucher. Occasionally she wore sexy lingerie for me, but this was very different, nothing like I'd expected. My wife is a very sexy woman, and we enjoy ourselves in the bedroom. We've played around with sexy singles and occasionally couples as well, but I'd never experienced something quite like this. How she thought of this unique birthday gift, I wasn't sure, but I was intrigued by her creativity.

I knew that she'd been up to something for about a week, but I had absolutely no idea what she had in store for me.

She liked to tease me, often without me knowing. Now some of her quirky behavior made sense. She'd definitely been lining things up in fours around our house for a few days, and mentioning friends of hers that I was certain I'd never heard of. I pretended not to notice the curious queues of items. I didn't think too much of the names at the time, because she did have a wide circle of friends and often made new acquaintances when she was out and about at various classes and activities. She was always up to something new and interesting; however, I never suspected that the names she mentioned belonged to three very sexy women with very pretty pussies that were all mine for the night.

She didn't give me a ton of notice of what was happening for my gift, and at first when she told me I thought she was being silly, teasing me. After all, having four women as my sexual playthings for the evening was something many men can only dream of, yet here was my wife actively encouraging it and even participating herself.

It only became real to me when, at six pm on the dot on my very special day, the doorbell rang. She went to answer it, while I was still getting ready in our bedroom. I peeked out the window and saw that there were indeed three women standing at the door. I couldn't see them in detail and I didn't want to stare–there'd be time for a very close-up view later–but they all had long hair, some wavy, some straight, and seemed to be wearing a variety of outfits that wouldn't look out of place going for dinner at a nice restaurant. I heard her let them in and the friendly chit-chat of female acquaintances ricocheted from the kitchen down to the bedroom where I was finishing getting dressed.

A few minutes later, my phone buzzed and my wife had texted me. *We're ready for you*, it said. I felt a mild throbbing in my groin, but still kind of needed to see things to believe it. Part of me, in the very back of my head, thought she might have been messing with me and these were friends who she merely invited around for book club or something.

When I reached the kitchen and adjoining living room, I soon realized that I had nothing to worry about. This was for real. Three very attractive women, all very different, were waiting for me, and none of them were wearing much. Each wore lacy lingerie, and they were all enjoying a glass of champagne. My wife offered me a champagne flute when I entered the room and I took it. I greeted the group and went to sit with them on the couch, where we exchanged small talk. The conversation flowed, as if they weren't sitting there in their sexy lingerie, about to give themselves over to me.

I couldn't help but take in each of them in an appreciative gaze, up and down. One of them had long dark hair that cascaded about her shoulders in sexy waves. She was curvy and firm, with breasts and hips that hit in a way that made my pants tighten thinking of the possibilities. The second had medium-length blonde hair, parted to the side, that cascaded around her face. She had smaller, perky breasts that exposed hard nipples that I couldn't stop looking at and had the strong urge to tweak.

The third woman was slim but muscular, and I could tell she worked out. Her hair was shorter, more severe. There was something pleasing about her svelte, athletic body that made me instantly drawn to her, and I couldn't wait to fondle her pretty ass that was peeking out the bottoms of her lace panties.

'Well, this is my husband. And here is your gift,' said my wife. 'As you all know, we're here to give him a stack, so let's get started.' They all eyed my groin, my pants tight as my cock, incredibly hard by now, bulged against the fabric. They seemed hungry, and so was I.

With that, the four sexy women moved over to the large daybed at the end of the room. The four women, including my wife, began to undress each other in front of me, bras and panties falling to the floor. My goodness, they were so fucking hot. Legs and breasts and hips and ass on display as they disrobed. They then climbed onto the day bed and had obviously planned which order they were going in, because before much time had passed they were all lined up in a row, my wife on top and the other three women beneath her.

This was a beautiful scene–four women lying on top of each other, legs spread. They revealed their four immaculately landscaped pussies in a stack, glistening, ready for me to fuck and lick and plow and fondle and do whatever I wanted with. We'd briefly talked boundaries when they first walked in, and they were clear that nothing was off limits today, they were mine for the taking.

I started to lick my wife's pussy and noticed that she was very wet. It was clear that I had turned her on with this very unique fantasy playing out, her in a lead role. This was just about the sexiest treat I could have imagined getting from my wife. I needed to make her feel wonderful, extremely satisfied in return. How giving of her to give this to me. So I teased her pussy, enjoying the smooth feel of her skin and inserting it within her, tasting her sweetness.

It was only fair that I also showed the same level of gratitude to the other women who had made my birthday gift possible. I moved downward, connecting my tongue with the next woman down. Her pussy was also wet, hungry for me. I'd seen her looking at me hungrily before, licking her lips, and now was my time to lick hers. I stuck my tongue deep within her pussy and felt her tremble in enjoyment, causing the entire stack of sexy ladies to move slightly. I lapped at her for a while, feeling her pussy wrap around my tongue in pleasure. She tasted wonderful, sensual, and I could have kept eating her out for hours, but that wouldn't have been fair to the rest of the ladies, so I continued my journey down.

The third woman had a rock-hard ass, stacked nicely in between two of the others. Her pussy was incredibly tight, and it enveloped my tongue so firmly I couldn't wait to see what it did with my cock; I almost certainly would find out very soon. I caressed her pussy up and down with my long tongue, taking care to reach a little lower and tease her clit. She too, moaned with pleasure. I was fascinated by the hardness of her ass and I couldn't help myself, as I found myself spreading her asscheeks and flicking my tongue against her asshole. She moaned. As I returned the attention of my tongue back to her pussy I slid my little finger inside her ass, slowly inserting it, and then pulling it in and out, in and out. I imagined what it would feel to have my hard cock inside her little ass and I felt my groin pulsate with desire at the mere thought. I continued to lick her clit and finger her. I wouldn't mind having a little bit of time just with this one gorgeous woman, later. But they were all sexy, so it was hard to pick just one.

Finally, I reached the bottom of this sexy little stack. This strong woman, holding the weight of three other beautiful ladies above her. I gave extra attention to her sexy little hole, licking and lapping at it while she shuddered and moaned. I wanted to make sure that just because she was placed at the bottom she didn't miss out on the same level of attention. I intended to make my way back up the stack with my mouth, so I spent double the time on this beautiful pussy, licking and nibbling on her clit. I inserted two fingers inside of her pussy, finger-fucking her while I continued to lick her. She came, her wet pussy pressed against my tongue, causing the whole stack of sexy women to wobble. A guy could get used to this variety of playthings; so many little details to pay attention to. All of these gorgeous women, here for me, to pleasure my cock and do whatever I desired. I felt the need to impress all of them, both in the moment and for the longer-term. What if this type of attention could become a regular thing?

I gradually made my way back up the stack, licking each pussy tenderly, sensuously, and engaging in some slow and gentle tongue-fucking. Each woman would moan and I could tell they were enjoying my expert pussy-licking abilities. My wife had trained me well, and my regular efforts to please her were evidently paying off with this expanded audience. I loved the way each women tasted and smelled, their own unique signature, and I enjoyed how wet they all were, finding this sexy situation made them as horny as I was.

I finally made my way up to the top after my little pussy-licking expedition down the stack and back up again. None of them could say I hadn't treated them well. Two of them definitely came as a result of my tongue, and the others were clearly on the verge. I was impressed that the stack had remained intact. I could only think that by taking the time to pleasure them individually, to make them as wet and hot as possible for me, the possibilities for what they'd let me do to them were endless. I fully intended to make the best use of this evening as I could, with these four beauties in my home, my wife encouraging me to fuck and lick and fondle and tease in whatever way I saw fit. After all that licking, I was ready for some fucking. My girthy cock was rock hard and wanted to plow all four of these beautiful pussies.

Conveniently, my wife's legs spread out around about my waist height, slightly lower, and I was able to grab her legs and enter her from behind. The stack of ladies swayed as I inserted myself into her wet pussy, thrusting slowly, her wetness enveloping me. She felt wonderful, familiar but in a way that emphasized what a lucky man I was; tight, and pleasurable. Some men would kill to have a pussy like hers on tap, and here she was letting me sample several others at the same time.

Again, I moved my way down the pile of gorgeous beauties, this time with my cock instead of my lips. I was so hard, throbbing with desire to try all of these women who I had just tasted. I wanted to be inside each of them, conquering them with my rock hard cock. They seemed to enjoy it, moaning as I slid inside them, taking turns to thrust in and out of each of them. In and out, in and out, sliding, sensually. I couldn't fuck them too hard from this position–I'm not a monster after all, and they were stacked so delicately atop each other–but I wanted to get a little rougher, so I knew we had to switch things up. As anticipated, the woman in the middle with the rock-hard ass had a pussy that wrapped firmly around my girth, enveloping me in a tight squeeze, clamping down as I thrust in and out.

Once I had completed the journey of my cock, up and down between these incredibly sexy women, I decided it was time for them to please me with their mouths. After all, it would be rude of them not to return the favor. I let them know that it was time to dismantle their stack, and it was time for each of them to show me what their tongues could do, both individually and as a group. Time for some sucking and licking for me. I'd only ever received a blowjob from one woman at a time before, so this part of the night was just one in a series of pleasurable experiences that was a first. My wife had let me have another woman suck my cock before while she watched, on more than one occasion, but the sheer quantity of mouths I was about to have pleasuring my dick was new for both of us, and I for one could not wait.

I sat on the edge of the bed and I leaned back, dick standing tall and proud and ready for the next part of our session together. I couldn't help but eye each of their mouths, their voluptuous lips that were about to pleasure me one by one. Each of them approached me, one after the other, sucking on my cock. Two of them licked my hardness at once, making eye contact with me as their eyes bulged as they took in my girthy cock. I let my hips thrust back and forth rhythmically, as they enveloped me with their voluptuous lips and tongues. Pleasureful sensations rippled through my body as they licked and sucked, licked and sucked, over and over again. Once they had all had a turn, I decided it was time for each of them to take a ride.

They each stood in a line, single-file. All naked, and sexy, and hungry for my cock–good thing I was just as hungry for them. I was very ready to fuck. The first approached me and I guided her to straddle me. We lined her up with my rock-hard cock and I slammed her down hard. She began to ride me, ass slapping against my thighs. I tweaked at her nipples, pinching them hard and she cried out in pleasure as she continued to slide her pussy up and down, up and down, over me.

The other women took turns and I enjoyed the different sensations each of their pussies gave my cock as they rode me, each having a slightly different pace and rhythm and scent. I enjoyed looking into their eyes, at their tits, at the other women making eye contact while I fucked each of their friends one by one. By the time I had been ridden by the fourth women for a while I found myself coming inside of her in a rush of pleasure and adrenalin. I grabbed her ass in my hands and squeezed extremely tightly as I unloaded inside of her. The other women looked on, knowing they'd collectively got me to this point.

It was time to leave, my gift was done. The women put their clothes back on, engaging in small talk and smiling and laughing. They had clearly had just as much fun as me–well, almost as much fun, most likely. My wife and I saw them out, giving each one a hug and a kiss on their way out the door.

'How did you know this is exactly what I wanted? I didn't even know I wanted this!' he laughed, and his gaze turned lustful. 'But I did. I really, really, really wanted this.' He grabbed my ass and pulled me towards him in a long slow kiss. 'Thank you so much for making this happen, babe. I'll be thinking about it for a long time. We even have photo proof.' I kissed him back. 'I'm so glad you liked it. Want to show me how much you liked it?'

'Yes, I'd like to show you some of my appreciation. I think I'll be demonstrating my gratitude for this one for a long time to come.'

He shoved me backwards, onto the bed and yanked my legs apart firmly, exposing my pussy which was soaking as I'd been very excited to participate in his sexy little gift. He dove headfirst towards my pussy and I held onto his head as he lapped up my pussy juices, hungrily. The other ladies had gotten a little taster of his tongue action, but now his tongue was all mine. He licked and twirled, sticking it out so he could insert it inside me. In and out, left and right. He then centered his focus on my clit which he twirled around with his tongue and then began to lick up and down, rapidly, faster and faster until I found myself release all of the pent-up tension in my body in a fiery orgasm, pleasure ripping throughout my body and causing me to arch my back as I slammed his face into my pussy while he continued to lick me until I squirmed. I moaned in pleasure as my limbs relaxed. He looked up at me and smiled. I returned his smile and immediately flipped over onto all fours, facing away from him, my bare pussy exposed to him at the edge of the bed. He immediately slid his hard cock deep inside me. I cried out as he pounded me, very hard, over and over again, just the way he knew I liked it. The headboard hit the wall as he thrust in and out of me, his hands firmly grasping my hips, as he controlled me, owned me. He then came, too, pulling himself deep inside me as he moaned in pleasure.

THE END

She serves them every day.
Now it's time for them to
return the favor.

Banging the Barista

A sexy FFM menage story

M.C. Plains

Story Three: Banging the Barista

My husband is attracted to sexy young women. In their twenties, with their perky tits and tight asses. It used to bother me, especially as I evolved into my thirties and beyond. But now I see it as a bit of an advantage. My husband and I have enjoyed sexy dalliances with various singles and occasionally couples, and if anything it's magnified our sex life, adding a degree of pleasure and satisfaction that I never thought possible. That's not to say anything was wrong with it before; we were adventurous, and genuinely enjoyed time together in the bedroom and various other locations, but there's something about adding a nubile young woman into the mix, and watching your husband doing all sorts of things to her, that's an incredible turn-on. One of our favorite things to do is reflect back on our fantasies that we've acted out. It's like we've made a mental album that we flick through together. It makes us very aroused, even when it's just the two of us together, from simply thinking about it.

We hadn't had one of our intimate rendezvous for a little while, a couple of months maybe. Too busy with work and looking after our kids and the house. We'd recently renovated our kitchen, adding in a large kitchen island. We liked to cook and do other things on it when the kids weren't home. We'd also had a special area built in our house where we sometimes liked to invite people over for a little... bedroom fun, that wasn't in a bedroom. But we were flexible about where our little escapades took place, and we liked to mix things up. It's nice to have options about who you fuck and where you fuck, after all. These renovations had swung us out of our regular routine and took up a ton of time on top of our regular work day. We knew that they'd be well worth it, but it meant that we hadn't been focused on any sexy adventures recently, and it felt like it might be about time to do something to spice things back up again. Not that things were going badly in the bedroom department by any means–I was still having a lot of fun with my husband. But sometimes we just wanted someone else to join in; we liked having our little playthings.

One thing that we had kept up during this busy time is our need to be thoroughly caffeinated at all times, and that involved a twice-daily visit to our local coffee shop. It was located just down the street, on the corner. And they had recently hired a new barista. I could tell that my husband thought that Sarah was sexy. I watched his eyes checking out her cute little ass as she bent over to pick up cups and saucers. As she leaned towards him to hand him his order, his eyes would skim her ample cleavage. She was always showing just enough to pique his interest, to get his attention. I don't think she did it on purpose; she would have looked cute and sexy wearing just about anything as far as I was concerned, but she really did just have an effortless way about her. An energy and a charisma that was palpable just by ordering coffee from her and being in her presence for a couple of moments. I also observed the way that they'd make eye contact when he'd order. She was just doing her job, one might think, but they seemed to have a spark between them. She was always very friendly towards me as well, complimenting what I was wearing and chit-chatting about my day.

'That Sarah girl at the coffee shop is nice, isn't she?' I said to my husband one morning, as he was reading the news on his phone while we had breakfast. I wondered if he'd pretend not to know who I was talking about.

'The sexy barista? Yes, she's very nice.' He wiggled his eyebrows at me and grinned. He knew he didn't need to play games with me, hide his attraction. Some might find it disrespectful but I appreciated how my husband could be forthright about his desire, his pervy ways. I'd rather my husband openly ogle a sexy young woman in front of me than do something foolish behind my back.

'I've seen you staring at her ass and her tits. You're not the most subtle about it. I think she is interested in you as well.'

'Oh really?' he said, putting his phone down. 'What are you thinking?'

'It's been a while since we invited a new friend over. I think she's very attractive myself. She's shown up in a couple of very hot dreams I've had recently, and while the dreams were good I can only imagine it would be more delicious to play with her in real life. Maybe we can try to assess her interest next time we go for coffee?'

'You always have the best ideas,' he said.

Later that day, we went for our usual mid-afternoon coffee. We both worked from home and liked to escape for half an hour or so and chit-chat while we recaffeinated. We weren't the types that would stop drinking coffee in the afternoon. We were risk-takers, adventurous in the bedroom and also with our coffee consumption. Plus, it meant we got to see Sexy Sarah from the coffee shop again. And see if she was interested in joining us for a sexy romp.***

We headed into the coffee shop at our regular time, and it was still pretty busy. Many of the tables and chairs were full of people enjoying their afternoon beverage of choice, reading books and scrolling through their phones. Top of the charts music played fairly loudly in the background mixed in with the distinctive sounds of coffee being ground and milk being frothed, creating a buzzy ambience. Sure enough, Sarah was there, making coffee for the customers in front of us. This little delay in getting to speak with her gave us the opportunity to check her out another time. She was wearing ripped denim shorts and a tank top with a few buttons at the top, which had been undone to reveal her signature cleavage. Her outfit was simple, but accented her slim waist and her shapely legs. It was different looking at her knowing that we were going to invite her to get naked to us. While I'd always had a bit of a perv at her when I was getting a coffee, I felt a little bit nervous this time, knowing we were going to be asking her to get frisky with my husband and me. I looked at my husband and he winked at me, excited about what we were about to do.

The people in front of us seemed to be taking an excruciatingly long time to select their drinks. They had questions about several items on the menu, and it took what seemed like forever before they made a suggestion. They then proceeded to select several baked goods, discussing the nutritional content of each one and gradually narrowing it down until they made a decision. I rolled my eyes as they then argued over who was going to pay, and then one of them got into a panic when they realized they couldn't find their debit card. Literally the worst people to be in front of you when you're trying to summon the courage to chat up the barista and invite her home to have a threesome with you, engage in a bit of a menage. If I hadn't been so anxious about what we were about to do, I probably would have laughed at the comedy of it all.

Finally, after what seemed like an entire ice age, time for me to get nervous and worry she might turn us down, we got to the front of the line. 'Hey there,' she said, smiling at us with white teeth and sparkling eyes. 'The usual for both of you?'

'Actually, we're thinking of trying something new,' said my husband. 'What's your favorite thing on the menu?'

She responded quickly, one of their signature beverages that was blended and topped with whipped cream. 'Oh, you like whipped cream? Good to know.' I had visions of licking whipped cream off of her body and felt myself blushing at the thought. She laughed, 'Yes, I like the way it melts into the coffee, it's very creamy and delicious.'

'Well, how could we turn that down. We'll take two of those please. Thank you for the recommendation.'

'Of course, I'm happy to help you!' she flicked her hair back, revealing one side of her neck which was sexy and slender.

I almost chickened out at that point, as she busied herself making drinks. It would have been easy to make an excuse, to say that there were too many people in the coffee shop who could potentially overhear, or who knew the dirty thoughts running through our minds. But I really wanted to treat my husband, and I knew this was exactly what he wanted.

'What time do you finish?' I asked. 'I'm not trying to be weird or anything but, uh... we really appreciate how kind you always have been to us when we come in here.'

'You're two of my favorite customers. I'm glad my service pleases you. That made my day,' she smiled.

'Well, I guess I'll be direct in that... we'd love to return the favor. We'd like to invite you over to our place for a meal, and a few drinks.'

'That actually sounds really fun,' she said. 'I'd like that. I'm new to the area and don't know many people. I'd love to spend some time with you both.'

'When works for you? We're wide open.'

'I have plans tonight. How's tomorrow?'

'Perfect, why don't you come around at 630?'

'Works for me,' she said. Her eyes flicked over to my husband and she gave him a curious look, intense. She may have been undressing him with her eyes, as women often did. I hoped that's what she was doing.

The next 24 hours went extremely slowly. I had lots of things to do, but my mind kept focusing on what was going to happen the following evening. Sarah, the sexy lady from the coffee shop, was going to be in our home. And she was going to fuck my husband. I was so excited. I wanted to play with her as well, of course. Despite us usually going to the coffee shop a couple of times a day, we decided it would be better to stay away the next morning and afternoon, skipping our visits. It seemed like we should leave her alone while she worked, because she was going to be getting plenty of attention later, from both of us, when she came to our home. I was worried as well that if we spent too much time at the coffee shop that day she might chicken out for some reason, think that we were following her around. I mean, we had checked her out several times and then invited her over for some bedroom shenanigans, but I didn't want her to think we were going full-on creeper status. So in an effort to maintain some degree of mystery, to not let on that my husband and I were salivating over the idea of fucking her later in the day, we decided to stay away. No sneak peeks. We'd see plenty of her later.

The time crawled by. 12pm. 2pm. 3pm. Finally, evening rolled around. I made sure that I cleansed my body and slathered myself in a moisturizer, spraying myself with a sexy perfume. My legs were smooth and freshly shaved, as was my pussy. I wanted Sarah to enjoy in me the softness that contrasted so nicely with my husband's hard angles. I dressed myself in a white dress–ironic, considering what we were going to be doing was anything but innocent. It showed off my own figure, which was pretty decent if I do so myself. My husband appreciated the way I kept myself in fantastic shape for myself, for him, and for the people we liked to enjoy in the bedroom together. I wore teardrop-shaped earrings and some other subtle jewelry, not wanting it to get caught on or scratch anything. There was going to be a lot of exposed skin, a lot of delicate areas, after all.

At 630pm, my husband and I were standing in the kitchen, freshly showered and dressed. He looked handsome in an ironed button up shirt with the two top buttons undone, revealing a glimpse of his muscular chest. He wore jeans and some trendy shoes. His hair was parted at the side and he looked like he could have been going out to a nice restaurant for dinner. Which made sense because he would be eating soon, that was for sure. Ten minutes went past, and then fifteen, and I started getting a bit worried.

'She'll be here soon, I'm confident,' said my husband.

'Are you sure we gave her the right address?'

'Yes, stop fretting. She's going to come.'

'Oh, I'll make sure of it,' I said.

Sure enough, a couple of minutes later the doorbell rang. I peeked through the peephole and it was Sexy Sarah from the coffee shop.

'Sorry I'm late,' she said. 'I had a long shift and wanted to go home to shower and change.'

'Not a problem at all. Here, give me your coat and go and put your feet up, working so hard. We'll make sure you get to relax tonight.'

Sarah looked gorgeous. She was wearing a sexy dress, a style of outfit that we hadn't seen her wearing while at work. It had a plunging neckline revealing her delicious-looking breasts, and a short hem. I loved her confidence, the way she embraced being a millimeter from her butt sticking out of most of her outfits. She wore strappy, elegant heels that showcased her painted toes and her muscular calves.

My husband helped Sarah remove her coat and he hung it up in the hallway while I escorted her into our living room which was ready for a visitor. Candles burned softly in the corners and we had our bar set up for cocktails. I gestured to our comfy couch and Sarah took a seat.

My husband followed us into the room and we all chit-chatted. I couldn't stop staring at Sarah and neither could my husband. She was very attractive in a cute, sexy way. 'Do you want to take your shoes off and put your feet up? I'd love to give you a foot massage, work out those knots from your shift?'

That sounds lovely, she said, and bent over to undo her sandals, revealing a further glimpse of her cleavage.

'Let me,' said my husband. 'I'd be more than happy to help.'

He moved over to her and knelt down, undoing her sandals and removing them one by one. He proceeded to massage her feet. My husband gave wonderful foot rubs, and I'm sure it felt amazing given she'd been standing all day at work.

'Oh, wow, that feels amazing,' said Sarah, as my husband needed the balls of her feet, the bridges of her feet and her heels. She smiled and he made eye contact her while he worked. 'I just want to make you feel good, after all you do for us every day,' he said, smiling back.

Once he was done with the massage, instead of going back to the armchair he'd been sitting at previously, he sat on the couch with Sarah. 'Why don't you come over here, too?' she suggested, patting the space on the couch on the other side of her. I happily joined them, each of us framing her between us. 'So,' she said. 'I meant it when I said you were two of my favorite customers. I'm always excited to see you when you come in.'

'We're always excited to see you as well, when we come in,' said my husband. Cautiously, he placed his hand on her thigh. 'Do you mind if we show you how much we appreciate you, and all of the hard work you do for us, each and every day?'

I placed my hand on her other thigh. 'We'd really like to demonstrate our appreciation, if that's okay with you.'

She nodded. 'I'd like that a lot,' she said.

My husband pulled down Sexy Sarah's sleeves and lowered her dress, exposing her bare breasts. He lifted one into his hands and kissed it, licking her nipple with his outstretched tongue. I mirrored him, lifting her other breast and enjoying the feel of its weight in my hand. I proceeded to lick and nibble at her other nipple, and she moaned in pleasure.*********

'I'd like to watch you together,' he said to us, and we smiled at each other. We moved forward and started to kiss, gentle and passionate, our mouths and tongues grazing each other, exploring. Sarah reached over and ran her hand over my husband's thigh. His pants were tight, the bulge growing as he watched us make out.

He reached over to me and had me turn around so he could unzip my dress. I stood up and it fell to the floor, leaving me completely naked. It hadn't made sense to wear underwear tonight, so no sexy lingerie this morning. Just straight-up tits and pussy. I knew my husband found those sexy and I hoped that Sarah did, too. Immediately I had my answer, as she gazed at me, licked her lips and told me I was fucking hot. 'The feeling is mutual,' I assured her. I removed her dress, pulling it down over her hips and off her feet, as well as her panties.

I moved her thighs apart and my husband and I both looked at her pussy from where we were sitting. It was pink, pretty, and I could tell it was starting to become very wet. Just the way we liked it. He reached a hand over, not wanting to wait, and began to stroke her with his fingers, very gently at first. She moaned with pleasure. He inserted two fingers inside her and let them move in and out of her, slowly, and she arched herself towards him, enabling to reach in more deeply. I removed my husbands fingers and proceeded to lick them one by one, enjoying the way that she tasted. I let him take his hand back–I wanted to taste her directly now. I pulled her thighs further apart and extended my tongue, and proceeded to eat this sexy young woman's pussy while my husband watched. I used my tongue in many ways, sliding it deep inside of her and thrusting in and out, emulating what my husband's fingers had been doing just moments ago. I used it to focus on her clit, twirling it about as she bucked and gyrated against my mouth. I slid it up and down the fully length of her pussy, and knew by the way that she moaned that I was generating many different sensations of pleasure throughout her body.

My husband leaned over and unzipped his pants, allowing his cock to unfurl from his underpants, tall, erect and girthy. She glanced at it appreciatively, clearly impressed by what he had to offer. She leaned over and placed his cock in her mouth and proceeded to lick and suck, allowing him to penetrate her mouth over and over again. I could hear her saliva moving about his cock as he thrust into her, her lips enveloping his hardness.

My husband decided he wanted to taste her as well and had her lean back, her back on the far arm of the couch. He pulled her legs apart roughly and went in hungrily with his tongue, devouring her pussy like he hadn't had a meal in weeks. 'Fuck you taste good,' he said. She moaned as he increased his pace. He inserted two fingers again into her, and thrust them in and out while he paid attention to her clit with his talented tongue. In and out, up and down. She bucked against him and reached out and held one of my breasts as she came hard, her other hand pulling his head onto her pussy. He lifted his head up as her orgasm subsided, leaned over to me and we engaged in a long, slow tongue kiss while Sarah watched.

He then pulled me up to him on the couch and I inserted his girthy cock inside me as I straddled him, riding him up and down. Sarah laid back and watched, a lazy and satisfied smile on her face as she watched me fuck my husband. 'I knew it would be hot to watch you fuck, I could tell from the first time you came into the coffee shop,' she said, as my husband's cock repeatedly slammed deep inside me and I moaned out loud at the sensations racing through my body.

'Oh yeah? You want me to fuck you as well?'

'Oh yes please,' she said.

My husband had me hop off him and immediately leaned over and climbed on top of Sarah. He held her arms down and thrust deeply inside of her. She cried out in pleasure. He rammed himself into her, forget the gentle stuff. He wanted it rough and she seemed to enjoy it as he slammed into her pussy with his rock hard cock, over and over again until he came, his whole body shuddering as he groaned in pleasure, tension releasing from his body as he spilled into her.

As she got dressed, I took some final looks at her gorgeous body. 'Well, you've given us a whole new thing to think about when we go to the coffee shop. We hope it doesn't get... awkward when we come in for our coffees each day.'******

'Oh far from it,' she said. 'I'll look forward to your visit, and I'd quite like to come and visit you both again soon.'

'It depends, are we still some of your favorite customers?'

'You've officially become my absolute favorite customers,' she giggled.

We all smiled, and we gave her a kiss as she left the house. 'See you soon, Sexy Sarah from the coffee shop,' my husband said as he waved.

My husband turned around and said, 'Get your ass on the couch, right now.' I wasn't going to even try to complain. He followed me as I raced to the couch and threw my legs open. He licked at me briefly, sending ripples of energy pulsating throughout my body and, not able to wait any longer, he buried his girthy cock deep inside of me, thrusting in and out the way I'd watch him do to the sexy young woman from the coffee shop just a bit ago.

Once we were both finished, he turned to me. 'Should we give that coffee shop a break for a week or two, keep her on her toes?'

'Yep, there's another one down the street. Let's see what's going on there. Might get a little roster of sexy baristas going.'

'This is one of the many reasons I love you, dear,' said my husband. 'You're up for so many little fun adventures. I'll never get tired of you my sexy wife.'

'Likewise,' I grinned at him.

We headed to bed and he held me in his arms. I knew that he would probably wake me in the night to fuck me again while he reminisced about plowing into Sexy Sarah from the coffee shop. And that was fine with me, I'd also be thinking about her and the way she tasted. Two could play this game. And I was in it for good.

THE END

Also By M.C. Plains

Visit my Author Central page to find all new releases.
Join my newsletter for the latest info on new releases:
https://subscribepage.io/Gkj4yZ

Novellas

Dara's Story: The Nanny Moves In

Nanny with Benefits

Short Stories

A Babysitter for My Birthday

Yearning for the Yoga Instructor

Seducing the Server

Unintended Playthings

A Gift for My Husband

Banging the Barista

Stack of Pleasure

Inviting the Babysitter

The Babysitter Brings a Friend

Dinner for Three

Ordering In

A Weekend with my Girlfriends

The Ice Cream Shop

Getting Freaky at the Tiki

Recipe for Seduction

Collections

Very Sexy Bedtime Stories: Hot Erotic Tales for Men & Wome

The Adventures Collection

The Arrangements Collection: A Satisfying Trio of Sexy Stories

The Hot Girl Summer Collection: A Trio of Sexy Stories

www.ingramcontent.com/pod-product-compliance
Lightning Source LLC
LaVergne TN
LVHW050348160826
845677LV00014B/3856

* 9 7 9 8 3 5 3 2 6 5 5 4 2 *